PETAL AND POPPY

The text of this book is set in Cheltenham.
The display type was hand-lettered.
The illustrations were created digitally.

The Library of Congress Cataloging-in-Publication Data
Jahn-Clough, Lisa.
Petal and Poppy / by Lisa Clough and Ed Briant.
pages cm. — (Green light readers)
Summary: Best friends Petal, a tuba-playing elephant, and Poppy,
an adventurous rhinoceros, do not always agree on what to do but
they can always count on one another when the going gets rough.
ISBN 978-0-544-11380-0 paperback
ISBN 978-0-544-11477-7 paper over board
[1. Best friends—Fiction. 2. Friendship—Fiction. 3. Elephants—
Fiction. 4. Rhinoceroses—Fiction.] I. Briant, Ed, illustrator. II. Title.
PZ7.J153536Pet 2014
[E]—dc23
2013020667

Manufactured in China
SCP 10 9 8 7 6 5 4 3 2 1

4500451499

PETAL AND POPPY

BY LISA CLOUGH AND ED BRIANT

HOUGHTON MIFFLIN HARCOURT
Boston New York

What if Poppy is bitten by a lobster?

Or swallowed by a whale?

What if a storm comes and carries her away?

9

I wish Petal could see this.

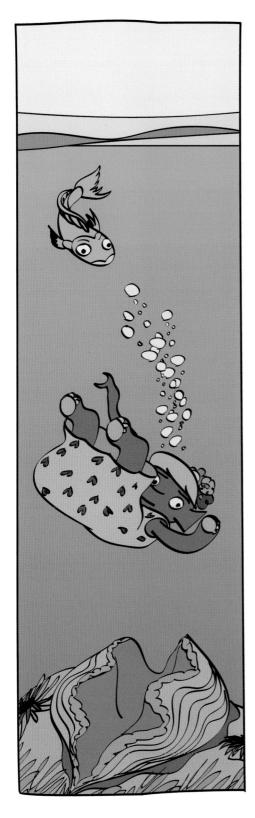

27